This edition is published by Derrydale Books,
a division of Crown Publishers, inc.
by arrangement with Award Publications Limited

abcdefgh

Printed in Belgium

Enid Blyton
The Five Little Elves

Illustrated by RENE CLOKE

DERRYDALE BOOKS
NEW YORK

THE FIVE LITTLE ELVES

ONE-BUTTON, Two-Button, Three-Button,
Four-Button and Five-Button were five
little elves who were so alike that no
one could tell which was which.

Because of this, one
of them wore only one button
on his tunic, the next had
two buttons, and so on – and everyone
called them by the number of their buttons.

"Here comes One-Button!"
the pixie-folk used to cry,
as they saw the elf with one
button coming down the road.
"Two-Button is out
shopping," they said,
when they saw the elf with two
buttons going out with a basket. It was
quite easy to tell which was which by
counting the buttons.

Now one day all five elves went out
together to picnic on Bumblebee Common.
One-Button carried the kettle,
Two-Button carried
the bread and butter,
Three-Button carried the cakes.

Four-Button
carried the apples
and Five-Button
carried the cups and plates.

Just as they were crossing over the little
bridge that leads to the common, Three-
Button stumbled and fell. He only just
managed not to fall into
the water beneath
– but alas, the
cakes did!

How upset all the
Button-Elves were!
It was dreadful
to have no cakes at a picnic tea.
Three-Button was very sorry about it, but
it couldn't be helped.

They found a nice place to have their picnic
and then Three-Button said that, as he had
lost the cakes, he would take the job of
going to ask for water in their kettle.
So off he started. He saw a cottage in
the distance and walked towards it. As
he drew near to it, he smelt a delicious
smell of newly made cakes.

He knocked on
the door and an
old woman opened it.

Three-Button thought
that she looked very much
like a witch, but she
had kind eyes, so he
felt sure that she
couldn't be.

"Please may I have some
water for my kettle?" he
asked. "Certainly," said
the old woman.
"Step into my kitchen and
take some from the faucet."

So Three-Button walked
into the kitchen and
filled his kettle.

Then he suddenly caught sight of the table
and his eyes and mouth opened in surprise-
for it was piled high
with hundreds of
cakes, all newly made
and smelling simply
delicious!

Three-Button remembered how he had dropped
the picnic cakes into the water and a very
naughty thought came into his head. Surely
the old woman would never miss five
cakes from such a big pile.

In a second
the naughty little
elf snatched five
buns from the
table, took up
his kettle and ran
out of the door.

He raced back to the others and showed them
what he had gotten – but he didn't tell them
that he had stolen them.

They were very pleased.

Soon the kettle was
boiling away merrily
and One-Button
made the tea.
Then the elves
set to work on the
bread and butter. When
they had finished that, they started on the
newly baked cakes. They were simply
delicious!
But just as they were handing one another
the apples, a curious thing happened.
Each elf began to feel very uncomfortable.

They looked at
one another and
then cried out
in dismay.
"We're all getting
very fat!"
they cried, and
pointed to each other.

Sure enough they were! Their little tunics
became very tight, and their toes burst out
of their boots. Their hats soon were much
too small and fell off their heads.
"What is it?" cried One-Button.
"What can be the matter with us?"

But none of them knew. It was really
dreadful. They grew bigger and bigger and
at last, with a pop, One-Button's little
button flew off his tunic! Then Two- Button's
two buttons flew off too, and Three-Button's and
Four-Button

Five-Button's popped off as well and soon
the grass was strewn with all their buttons

Crying bitterly they ran home. Everyone
they met stared at them in astonishment.
When they got home, they shut
themselves up and
looked all through
their magic books to
find out what was the
matter with them.

And very soon they
discovered that pimpernel
cakes eaten newly made
caused people to grow
terribly fat all in a hurry.
Then Three-Button
began to sob and he
confessed to the others that he had stolen
the five cakes he had brought to them.
"I expect they must have been pimpernel
cakes," he wept. "I remember seeing a lot
of pimpernels growing round the old woman's
cottage. Oh, whatever are we to do?"

"Wait a minute!" cried One-Button eagerly. "Here is a page that tells us what to do to get back to our own size again. Listen: "Melt salt and sugar together in a silver thimble and drink it in front of a fire. Then you will grow thin once more!""

It wasn't long before
all the elves were
solemnly drinking salt
and sugar from silver
thimbles in front of
their kitchen fire.

No sooner had they finished than they
suddenly shrank back to their ordinary size!
How glad they were! They took hands and
danced round and round in glee.

Just then a pixie friend of theirs came in
to see them.
"Oh," he said, "I just wanted to know if
Two-Button would – but, dear me, which of
you *is* Two-Button? You haven't any
buttons on at all and you're so alike that
I can't possibly tell which is which!"

The Button-Elves looked at each other.
Of course, the buttons had popped off their
tunics when they had grown so fat – and now
no one would know which was which! And to
make things much worse,
the elves themselves
couldn't remember
who had one button,
and who had two,
three, four and five.

"*Now* what are we to do?" asked the elves
in despair. "Who can tell us who is who?"
All the little folk of
the town came to try and
help them but, really, the
elves were so much alike
that it wasn't a bit of use.

"There is only one
person who could help
you and that is Dame
Pimpernel up on Bumblebee
Common," said a pixie.
"She is a very clever
person indeed." "That
must be the old woman
whose cakes we took,"
said one of the Button-
Elves.

"Well, we'd better go and confess, and
perhaps she will help us."

So off they all
went and soon
arrived at Mother
Pimpernel's cottage.
She was very
much surprised to see
them, and even more
astonished when she
heard that they had
stolen five of her cakes
and had grown so fat.
When she heard that all their buttons
had popped off, she laughed till the tears
ran down her wrinkled cheeks.
"Please don't laugh at us," begged the elves.
"We have managed to get thin again but, you
see, we don't know which of us is which now.
People say that you are clever and can tell
us."

"I can tell you easily enough," said old
Mother Pimpernel. "But you must do something
for me in return. You have certainly been
punished for the naughtiness of one of you
but I think you should be punished a little
more. The next time you will all remember
not to touch things belonging to other
people."

"What shall we
do for you, then?"
asked the Button-Elves
humbly.
"You can come and
feed my chickens for
me every day," said the
old woman. "I really
haven't time."

"Very well, we
will take it in
turns to come
every day,"
promised the
elves. "Now
do please tell us
which is which."
"Well, One-Button's button is gone, but his
one button-hole is not!" said the dame
with a laugh, and she hooked her finger
into One-Button's one button-hole.
"You are One-Button. Two-Button is the one
with two button-holes, of course, and
Three-Button the one with three.
Four-Button and Five-Button can easily find
themselves by counting *their* button-holes
too. What a lot of little sillies you are!
You could easily have thought of that for
yourselves."

Then the Button-Elves began to laugh.
"Ha ha!" they went. "He he! Ho ho! What
sillies we are! Thank you, Mother Pimpernel;
now we will go home and sew on our buttons
again. Tomorrow One-Button will come and
feed your chickens for you!"

Off they ran
and got out their
needles and thread.
They sewed on
their buttons and
then felt very happy,
for once again they knew
which of them was which.

Each day they take it in turn to feed
Mother Pimpernel's chickens. On baking-day
they smell the newly made cakes and see them
on the kitchen table – but you may be sure
that not one of the Button-Elves goes
near them!